Twist of Fate

TWIST OF FATE

Twist of Fate

A Thought-Provoking Short Story
For Each Day of the Month

Paul E. Linzey

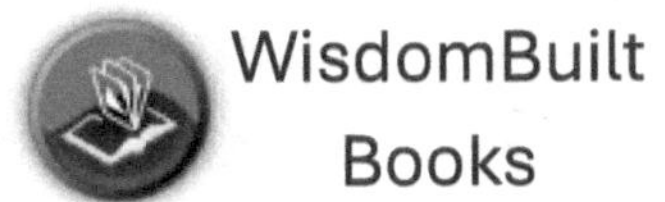

Twist of Fate

Twist of Fate is a work of fiction. All incidents, dialogue, and characters are products of the author's imagination, and are not to be construed as real. Any resemblance to real persons is entirely coincidental. The only exception is story 29.

The cover image is from Pixabay.com and is used by permission.

ISBN: 979-8-9985060-8-6

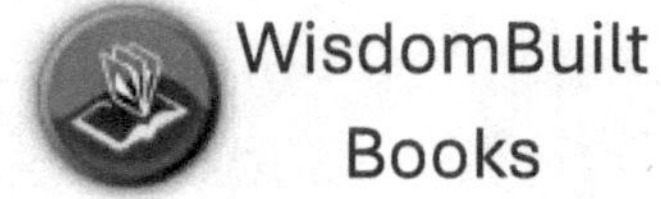

DEDICATION

To Jeff

My Son, My Friend

CONTENTS

1. One More Sunrise 1
2. A Gentle Nudge 5
3. Destined for Greatness 7
4. Mom's Flute 13
5. Vortex of Negativity 17
6. Black Ice 21
7. A Real Man 25
8. Seventeenth Question 29
9. Finally 33
10. Lovers' Island 35
11. One Warm Afternoon 37
12. Too Many Cons 41
13. Q & A 43
14. Beauty Queen 45
15. Self-Defense 47
16. Blue Bougainvillea 51
17. Superbowl MVP 53
18. Twist of Fate 55
19. It's In My Blood 59
20. Bananas 61
21. In-Laws 63
22. Dancing to the Music 67
23. Rumors 71
24. Life Sentence 75
25. Words of Hope 77
26. World's Best Burger 79
27. Engagement 83
28. If 85
29. Seeing Is Believing 87
30. The Coin 89
31. The Riddle 95

About the Author 101

Books by Paul Linzey 103

INTRODUCTION

Each February, Writer's Digest hosts a month-long event called February Flash Fiction Challenge. Every morning, managing editor Moriah Richard provides a writing prompt, and everyone participating writes a story in response. This book is a collection of my Flash Fiction stories.

I want to thank Writer's Digest for the daily story starters. My sons (Jeff, Kevin, and Chris) joined me in this year's February Flash Fiction Challenge. They and my wife commented, offered suggestions, or asked questions, all of which contributed to making the stories better.

By the way, Flash Fiction stories are typically no longer than 1,500 words and may be as short as the now-famous six-word stories, allegedly started by Ernest Hemingway.

Other than number twenty-nine, all of these stories are completely the figment of my imagination and are totally fictional. Twenty-nine was a real experience I had when I was nineteen years old.

Last year's collection of short stories is volume one in this series. *Twist of Fate* is volume two. And if you'd like to take a look at the stories that my sons wrote this year, they are collected in an anthology titled *Echoes from the Same House*.

I hope you enjoy the stories. If you do, please tell a friend about the book. I'd also appreciate a note or comment from you on my website, https://paullinzey.com/connect. And whether you like the stories or not, please go into Amazon and leave a review. Thanks.

Paul Linzey

TWIST OF FATE

1
ONE MORE SUNRISE

When James heard the news he just had to get out of the apartment and go for a run. He didn't know how much more bad news he could endure.

"It can't last forever," his friend told him.

"But what if it does?" he moaned.

Three hundred seventy-two days ago his dad died. Dad had been his best friend his entire life. One hundred twenty-nine days ago the company he had worked for the past eight years reorganized, and he had still hadn't found a new job.

Three days ago his fiancée dumped him. The entire four years they had been together she had talked about how great it felt to have found the perfect guy and the wedding was planned. But she met someone on a business trip and . . . well . . . that's history, now.

The phone call this morning told him the test results looked bad. To come in to the doctor's office at ten a.m. for the details.

"The negativity can't last forever," his friend told him.

"But what if it does?"

As he jogged the familiar route he remembered how it felt to have everything go right. Spending time with Dad. A job he loved, making good money. The love of his life by his side.

They listened to music, went on cruises, and watched movies. They did everything together. But what struck him at this moment was the way they enjoyed getting out early to see the sunrise. Sometimes over the water. Sometimes from a mountain top. Early morning break of dawn had always symbolized the start of a new day, a new era, a new beginning. And they loved planning their life together. Every day was new, always positive, always fresh.

But that life was over.

The medical news was worse than he expected. Cancer in his left elbow? How do you get that anyway? Preliminary results indicated it had already metastasized. They could only guess how much longer he had, and recommended surgery, then chemo. First on the list was to remove his left arm. James was left-handed.

Leaving the office, he realized he had some

important questions to consider. What would life look like? Did he want to go on living? Before he did anything, he wanted to experience one more sunrise.

2
A GENTLE NUDGE

As the tenth graders trudged into their science classroom, they saw the teacher lower the screen, turn on the projector, open YouTube, start a video, and then pause until it was time to watch. The class session was about animals giving birth in the wild.

She talked about lions in Africa, elephants in India, and shingleback lizards in Australia. Then she introduced the video, explaining that after giving birth to her calf, a mother humpback whale gives the newborn a gentle nudge to move it towards the surface because it has to breathe within fifteen seconds or it will drown. Then the teacher asked the class a question. Can you think of any ways human mothers help their babies survive?

Rather than brainstorming like she had hoped,

the students began grousing. My mother would never help me if I was dying, one girl sneered. Neither would mine, one of the boys replied. In fact, she's more likely to drown me. The majority of students voiced their agreement, laughing and jeering.

Then a shy kid in the back of the room raised his hand. Yes, Jamaal?

When I was five, I was in the basement with my dad. He was fixing the living room lamp because it needed a new cord and plug, and he was showing me all about it. My mom was also in the basement doing laundry when the washing machine overflowed and water covered the floor. My dad immediately jumped onto the workbench so he wouldn't be electrocuted but I was too little and couldn't climb up. Mom ran over, picked me up out of the water and sat me on the workbench. But she didn't make it. I miss my mom. If she was the whale in that video and I was the baby, I know she would push me to the surface. And I bet most of y'all's mothers would do the same.

3
DESTINED FOR GREATNESS

Jan loved singing and made the most of every opportunity. She sang in the church choir since she was four. Sang all the way through school. She had a music scholarship and sang in choirs and ensembles at the university. She had hoped to attend one of those prestigious conservatories after college, but always came up short and never got in.

For the past fifteen years, she was depressed, heartbroken, and embarrassed. Her family and all their friends had agreed, That girl is destined for greatness! But instead, she was a failure. The dream never came true.

In humiliation, she moved to a different state to start a new life. Got a decent enough job. Had a few friends. Dated once in a while. She still sang. In the shower, in the church choir, and at karaoke night over at Charlie's Steakhouse. Nobody in her world knew anything about her past. They knew nothing about her dream. Which really meant they knew nothing about her, and that carried its own kind of hurt.

One night she was watching "So You Think You Can Sing" on TV when the host, out of the blue, looked into the camera and said, Somewhere out there watching right now is someone who thinks your chances are over. Tell you what, if you can come to our studio in New York City on May first, I will personally give you another chance to fulfill your dream. So do whatever it takes to get here. Plan a fundraiser, empty your savings account, sell your very soul if you have to, but get here. This might be your last chance.

Jan sat up. It looked liked he was peering into her soul, as if she was the person he was talking to. Is it possible?

She had no savings. No idea how to do a fundraiser. But she did have a Soul. Aha! That's it! I will sell my Soul! How much will I need? Air fare, taxis, hotel, food, some new clothes. What else?

The day after putting the ad in Facebook Marketplace, a creepy, scary-looking man showed up at her apartment.

"I'm here to buy your Soul. Are you sure you want to go through with this?"

"Yes, I'm sure."

He handed her an envelope with the cash. She counted it.

"How do I know this isn't counterfeit?" she asked.

"Oh, it's real," he said as he turned to walk away.

"This is more than I advertised."

"Oh, but it's worth every penny. Trust me."

Jan knew she couldn't mess up this chance of a lifetime. She practiced. She searched through at least a thousand songs trying to select the one that would highlight her talents and her personality and put her in the best light. And when the day came, she was ready.

Since she didn't have a car, she Ubered to the airport. The flight was delayed a few hours, but she was going three days earlier than she needed to, just in case there were problems. Besides, the envelope contained more money than she had asked for in the ad. Maybe this was a good deal after all.

She loved New York: the restaurants, a Broadway show, the museums, the hustle and bustle of the city, the lights, even the subway. It all enchanted her. At a street corner, she met a nice-looking guy about her age, and he asked her out to dinner.

"Tell you what," she looked him in the eye trying to discern whether she should trust him. "Tomorrow I have an appointment. If that goes well, I'll meet you right here at this corner at 6:00 p.m. and we'll have dinner. But if it doesn't go well . . . well . . . . I'll probably not feel like it."

"It's a date. I think whatever you're doing will go

well. I just have a feeling about this. I'll be here tomorrow at six."

In the morning, Jan dressed but skipped breakfast because she was so nervous. Then she took a cab to the studio, where it seemed like a million people from all over the world had gathered. Every one of them assumed the guy on TV was talking to them. They all assumed this was their moment. And Jan immediately wilted. What chance did she have against all of them? Certainly there would be others with more talent, charm, or whatever they're looking for. Oh well. She'd come this far. Why not put her best foot forward.

When her name was called, the music started, and Jan walked on stage, closed her eyes, and sang. At the end of the song, they asked her to sing another. And another. And another.

"Jan, you are the person we've been looking for. The voice, the stage presence, the look, the whole package. We'd like to offer you a contract. What do you think?"

"Are you serious? This is what I've dreamed since I was a kid! Yes, I would like that. Yes. Yes. Yes!"

At ten minutes before six, she arrived at the corner. Her date was already there. He greeted her with a smile and they walked to a small café ten or eleven blocks away.

"So, what are you doing in New York?" he asked.

"It might sound silly, but I came for an audition at a studio."

"Ah, one of those?"

"Afraid so."

"But since you're here tonight, that means it went well, right?"

After a long pause, "Yes. It did. I can hardly believe it, to be honest."

"Congratulations."

"In fact, I'm moving to New York next month."

"Really? You mean, I might be able to see more of you?"

"If you're really as nice as you seem to be, perhaps."

"Perhaps?"

"Perhaps."

They sat quietly eating for a few minutes, each of them thinking and feeling and wondering about the other, silently falling in love.

"Would you like to hear how I came to be here this week?" she asked.

"Yeah, I would. What happened."

"Well, I've been a singer all my life, but never got the big break I was hoping for. I was watching the TV show when they announced this audition, and I wanted so badly to try one more time. But I didn't even have enough money to make the trip so I sold my car, came, and voila. Here I am."

"Wow! What a story. What kind of car did you have?"

"Small car. A Kia Soul. Red. I loved that car."

"Classic!" he chuckled.

"What do you mean?"

"You literally sold your Soul to come to New York."

They both started laughing.

4
MOM'S FLUTE

Phyllis didn't care about the money. It was nice, but that's not what mattered. She missed her mom. She missed hearing Mom talk. She missed Mom's music. So when she and her brothers met to read the will and divvy up the stuff, all she really wanted was Mom's flute.

She remembered lying in bed as a seven-year-old and falling asleep to the sound of arpeggios, melodies, and children's songs. Mom was a flutist in the local symphony and would often play what she called fluff pieces after the kids went to bed.

It was pretty cut and dried that everyone would get the same amount of money. But the simple will didn't discuss furnishings, jewelry, clothing, or art.

The house was to be sold and the proceeds split evenly. But what about the stuff?

Much of the discussion focused on the art because some of it was valuable—original oils, pottery, and bronzes. Her brother, John, had become an art dealer and knew the approximate value of each piece. Peter was a musician, but a cellist, so he didn't particularly care who got the flute. Fred was a real estate attorney and would handle the property sale. Phyllis was a history professor at the local state university. Her doctoral studies had focused on the transition of the Austrian Empire to the Austro-Hungarian Empire. But mostly, she missed her mom.

The siblings took turns declaring what they wanted, and the session was quite amicable. They all discussed what each item might be worth, but the value of the stuff was of pretty low importance. Each of them had other reasons for what they wanted: when and where Mom had acquired it, whether they liked it, and what it reminded them about Mom. And they all agreed that what they walked away with was final, there'd be no arguing later or fighting about who got what and what turned out to be worth more. Fred even provided the agreement for them all to sign . . . and they did.

A few days later, Phyllis's husband and kids were away for a few hours, so she took out her mom's flute. She wasn't a musician, but she had watched Mom so many times that she pretty much knew what to do, so she picked it up and blew into it. It seemed something was obstructing the airflow, so she looked into the end of the flute and found a rolled-up piece of paper.

Using a pair of tweezers, she pulled it out, trying not to rip whatever it was. Slowly, carefully, gently tugging at what seemed to be an old piece of paper. Finally, the whole scroll was out, a letter from her mother, accompanied by a small key.

My Dear Phyllis: I know how you enjoyed hearing me play when you were a little girl, so I hope you are the one reading this note. I love you so much and want you to have the instrument I played. In much the same way my music touched your heart, you are the music that touched mine. The key is to a safe deposit box at my bank. I wanted the contents to be yours because I think it will mean something to you. Whether you keep it, sell it, or give it away is entirely up to you. All my love, Mother.

On Monday, Phyllis's first class wasn't until early afternoon, so she took the key and went to the bank. There in the box was an original piece of music for flute: hand-written, signed, and dated by Ludwig Van Beethoven, 1815.

There was also a note: Receive this as a token of gratitude for your participation in and promotion of the Vienna Beethoven Society. The music is authentic. It has been certified by the Viennese Historical Society. The seal of the society was intact.

Phyllis cried and smiled and gasped all at the same time, and the bank manager standing at the door hurried over to see if she was all right.

5
VORTEX OF NEGATIVITY

When the staff met on Friday afternoons, they always ended up arguing and fighting. Name calling, criticizing, swearing, insulting. You name it. They were the epitome of a dysfunctional work group and everybody knew it. But nobody knew what to do or cared enough to do anything about it.

Mark had worked there about three years. At first, it bothered him and he tried to help steer the bickering in a more productive direction, but it's almost impossible to effect lasting change when the official leadership of the organization intentionally keeps things ugly and hurtful.

He had thought many times about leaving, just finding work elsewhere, but each time felt that would not be the best course of action. So when the meetings tended to get heated, he zoned out and did his best to ignore it, to varying degrees of success, of course. Some days he got sucked into the vortex of negativity and participated 100%.

Today, however, no matter what they did or said, regardless of what they literally threw at each other, he sat there with a grin and a faraway look in his eye as if he was daydreaming about being in Hawaii or some tropical island basking in the sun without a care in the world. And his demeanor bothered them.

"Mark! Wake up! Are you with us? Hello? What's the matter with you? Say something!"

Mark looked at them with that silly grin on his face and said nothing. Finally, the big boss couldn't take it anymore. He shouted in Mark's direction.

"Mark! What's wrong with you? Doesn't any of this matter?"

"No, sir. It does not. In fact, nothing you all are talking about, screaming about, bashing each other about matters at all."

"Is that so! And why are you so smug, self-righteous, and above it all?"

"Well, sir, it's like this. About a month ago, I was right here with you all, behaving exactly like every one of you are today. You know that. I've been here three years and fit right in, right? But I started feeling like I needed something more in my life. So I prayed and asked God if he was real to show me something, somehow. And he did. That night I had a dream about what it meant to have real peace inside. The next Sunday I went to a church near my house and I felt something stirring inside of me and I started to feel different. Like that peace in my dream was starting to be real in my mind and throughout my life. I told my girlfriend and she said she could see the change in me and wanted to experience it too, so she went to church with me. Last night she asked me to marry her and I said yes. So what we tend to argue about during these Friday staff meetings? Well, it really doesn't matter anymore. It's foolish and meaningless and doesn't accomplish anything. Look, I didn't come here to preach to you. In fact, as you could see, I tried real hard to say nothing. But since you practically ordered me to explain myself, boss, I decided to let you know. I don't condemn or judge any of you. But I really do feel like I have grown bigger than the pettiness we display in here week after week. Since I have to be here per your orders, sir, I will participate when we're actually talking about work, but when we devolve into immature, interpersonal, nasty stuff, well, I don't have to do any of that. I've come to love and care about everyone here and will be a friend, not anything else."

Everyone sat there in stunned silence. The boss sat there tapping on the conference room table trying to take in all that Mark had said. Then he spoke.

"What you said makes sense. I've noticed a change in you, too. In fact, if you're willing to make a commitment to stay a year, I'd like you to become my assistant and head up these weekly staff meetings. What do you think?

"Well, sir. This comes as a total surprise, but if you're willing to let me set the tone and make a few changes to how we do things, I just might be willing."

6
BLACK ICE

John was becoming frantic. Margo had texted him two hours ago saying her car broke down, the battery was dead, and she was out in the middle of nowhere on or near Murphy Road, or so she thought. She wasn't sure. No cars had driven by and there were no light anywhere, which made it pitch black. It had been snowing more than thirty minutes already and the temperature was dropping quickly.

It was now around twenty degrees and he still hadn't reached her. He wasn't sure if she had a coat and gloves, but one thing he knew for certain: not being able to start the car, she had no heater. And to make things worse, her cellphone had run out of power.

Even though he could no longer see street signs because of the heavy snow, he did have the GPS and it said Murphy Road was eighteen miles away. "God, I hope I get there I time." It wasn't really a prayer, more an exclamation and a wish. In fact, it had been far too long since he prayed. As he continued driving, he morphed his exclamation into a real prayer. "God, help me get there in time. My wife is lost and stranded. Help me find her." He even remembered to say "amen."

After driving a few more miles he came upon an accident. A police car had just arrived on the scene and one officer was helping the people whose car had hit black ice and slid into a ditch on the side of the road. The people weren't hurt and the car didn't appear to be damaged, fortunately. The other officer had placed a DETOUR sign on the road and was directing people to take an alternate route.

"No! I have to go straight ahead now! My wife's car is broken down a few miles from here and I have to get there."

"I'm sorry, sir. But we have to take care of this matter first. Besides, there's ice on the road for the next few miles. You'd be better off taking the detour."

"But I prayed." John was almost crying in desperation.

"Sir, I understand. I'm a firm believer in the power of prayer, too. So keep praying, but you have to take the detour. I'll be praying, too."

John turned right, as directed by the policeman.

Several other vehicles followed. The GPS said he was now on Jackson Road and that Murphy was more than an hour away. In these conditions, he had no idea how long it would take . . . if he could get there at all. At least there was another person praying. The officer did seem sincere, so maybe with two of them praying, he might get there in time.

As his car crested over a hill and descended on the other side, he lost control and began sliding. The cars behind him slowed and watched as he slid off the road into a gully, stopping about ten feet from another car that apparently had experienced the same fate. As he got out of the car to see if the other driver needed help, the door of the other car opened, and the driver walked towards him. The snow was so heavy that it was only when they got within five feet of each other that they recognized each other and embraced.

"You told me you were on Murphy Road," John shouted through the storm.

"I thought it was, but I couldn't read the sign very well."

"This isn't Murphy Road. It's pure luck that I found you here."

"Maybe not luck." Margo shivered her reply. "I've been praying."

Then John remembered that the officer also had been praying.

7
A REAL MAN

Andrew and Sara met at the mall food court on Saturday afternoon a few weeks before Christmas and both knew right away it was love at first sight. He moved into her apartment three days later and everything was great. Sara felt like the luckiest woman in the world to have found true love at age twenty-three.

Two days before Christmas, Adam told her he had invited a few friends over to celebrate.

"Wait a minute," she said. "You never talked to me about that."

"Well, I'm telling you now."

"It doesn't work that way, Adam. You ought to have the courtesy to talk to me before bringing people into my home."

"Hey, I'm the man here. I make the decisions."

When Sara disagreed, the discussion grew into an argument and Adam hit her and cursed.

"This isn't what love looks like," she blurted out.

He grabbed her by the arm, spun her around, and sneered into her face. "Well then, what do you think love looks like?"

"Love is patient and kind. Love is mutual respect, being there to serve each other, and help each other. But never forcing or imposing your will and demanding things go your way."

"You're kidding, right?"

"No, I'm not. If you don't know the basics about love, it was a tragic mistake to fall in love with you and ask you to move in."

Adam pushed her to the floor.

"And one more thing. Love never hits, hurts, insults, or disrespects." By now, Sara was crying.

He kicked her in the back and spat at her. Then he grabbed his jacket and keys and drove away.

Sara got up from the floor and drove to urgent care for an exam and then to the police station to file a report. The officer urged her to go to the county building and request a restraining order. After doing that, she needed time to think and sort things out so she went to her favorite restaurant, requested a booth in the back and ordered a club sandwich and a vanilla shake—her favorite comfort food.

As she was sitting there eating and thinking, Adam walked in and approached her.

"I've been following you all afternoon. Now get in the car. We're going home," he demanded.

"You don't live there anymore."

He grabbed her by the hair and began pulling her towards the exit when a man stepped in front of him and told him to let go of her.

"Get out of my way," Adam shouted.

"Dude if you think this how love works, you are sadly mistaken."

"So tell me, then. How does love work?" Adam snarled at the stranger who was an inch or so shorter. If it came down to a fight, he was sure he would win.

"Look, pal. Love is gentle and faithful. Love doesn't selfishly demand its own way. Love always honors the one you say you love. It's not being a bully or a tough guy. So I'm telling you one last time to let her go."

Adam let go of Sara's hair and took a swing at the stranger, who blocked the punch, grasped Adam's wrist, twisted the arm behind Adam's back, and used his leg in a sweeping motion to take Adam to the floor face down, his knee pressed firmly on Adam's back.

"One more thing," the stranger added. "Love protects and defends, it does not attack. A real man knows this, so obviously, you aren't a real man."

While holding Adam down on the floor, the stranger pulled out his phone, dialed 9-1-1, and asked for the police to come to the restaurant. A patrol car was in the area and got there pretty fast.

The restaurant employees and the dozen or so customers all gave the same eye witness report, and Adam was arrested.

The stranger walked over to Sara.

"Hi. I'm Andrew. Friends call me Drew. Are you OK?"

"Yes, thank you for stepping in when you did."

"You're welcome. Can I do anything else for you?"

"I can't think of anything."

"Well, here's my phone number if you ever need help or if you ever wanna talk. The police won't hold him very long. They'll ask you if you want to press charges. If you do, it might take a while for it to be settled, and you might be in danger, depending on what he decides to do, so be careful."

8
SEVENTEENTH QUESTION

"Grandma, how did you meet Grandpa?"

"How did it happen?"

"Sit down over there, grab yourself a big glass of lemonade, and close your eyes. Tell me when you're ready."

"Okay, Grandma. I'm ready."

I'll never forget it. When I was sixteen, I went to the county fair without a care in the world. I was young, energetic, full of life and hope. I'm still not sure why, but I woke up that day expecting something grand, something fantastic, something life changing. But more than that, I woke up expecting someone.

I had enough money to get into the fair and buy

a cola and a snack for lunch. But not enough to play any of the games or get a souvenir. Nothing like that. But for some reason, I had a hunch. A hunch that I would meet someone who would change my life. The strange part of my intuition was that it would be the seventeenth person who asked me a question. That's the person who would change the direction of my life.

The first question was at the entrance, "Do you want me to stamp your hand?" The second was a few minutes later, "Hey little lady, don't you want to try your luck at the ring toss?" And when I stopped for a drink of water, "Excuse me miss, can you tell me where the chicken exhibit is?"

I kept count of every question. Eight, nine, ten, eleven, and so on until sixteen. I just knew the next one would be magical. But nobody asked me any more questions. Not for a long time, and I began to doubt myself. I was sure there was going to be something special. I had dreamed of the number seventeen three nights in a row. And the third time convinced me. But something must have gone wrong.

I walked around the familiar places, visited the usual games and all the animal shows. When I went around the other side of the Ferris Wheel, there was a small boy sitting on a bale of hay crying. All by himself, nobody else around. Just sobbing. I kind of forgot all about my dream. I just wanted to help the little guy.

"Excuse me," I said. "Are you lost?

He just looked at me.

"Is there something I can do to help?"

"Can you help me find my brother?"

"Well, I can try. Why don't you stand up and hold my hand, and we'll go look for him."

The little guy must have been only three or four years old, but he stood up and took me by the hand.

"Let's go get you some cotton candy, and we'll just walk around til you see your brother, okay?"

He nodded. And that's what we did. Just walked around, not talking at all, sharing the cotton candy because I just had enough money for one. Walked around for almost an hour. Then suddenly I heard some guy holler, "Hey Buddy! Over hear! I've been looking for ya!"

The little boy yelled, "Jonathan!" and started running, right into the arms of a teenage boy who scooped him up and hugged him and kissed him, and I followed as fast as I could go. The little guy turned and pointed at me.

The older boy put Buddy down and came over to me. "I want to thank you for finding my brother and taking care of him."

"You're welcome," I smiled at him.

"I've been looking everywhere for the last hour or so and was ready to give up when I saw you through the crowd, and when you turned the corner, I saw Buddy holding your hand. I'd like to thank you for your kindness."

That's when it dawned on me. When the little boy asked if I could help find his brother, that was the seventeenth question I'd been asked at the fair.

"May I treat you to dinner and a few rides?"

Question eighteen.

"Umm, sure. I'd like that. But what about Buddy?"

"Oh, he'll be with us."

"Okay."

We spent as much time as we could together and six months later, on my seventeenth birthday, he asked me to marry him. Well, I had to get my pa's permission, but since Jonathan had a job by then, Pa said I could, and we've been married forty-two years now. I still can't figure it out, but for some unknown reason, I woke up knowing that question seventeen would change my life. I didn't know it would come from your Uncle Buddy. And I didn't know I would meet a boy who would later ask me to marry him, but it's been a grand, fantastic, and wonderful life.

"Wow, Grandma! I like that story."

"Me too, honey. Now give me a hug"

9
FINALLY

It took Nate three years to find a job.

For the past few months, he had been desperate.

No way of knowing how much longer

he could survive.

Or maintain his sanity.

Or fend off the bill collectors.

Now there was hope.

10
LOVERS' ISLAND

The invitations were sent two months ago. The venue confirmed weeks before that. The caterer delivered the food early. The preacher was there with the marriage license. The photographer was at the scene, the DJ already in full swing. Jeremy and Angela were ready to get married but something was wrong.

No guests or relatives? Not even their parents?

Jeremy walked out to the vacant parking lot. The normally busy boulevard was totally empty, not a single car going either direction. Then in the distance he noticed multiple plumes of smoke rising over the mainland, and another a little closer. He pulled out his phone, opened the news app, and saw the headline.

Bridge to Lovers Island Bombed
in Early Stages of War

11
ONE WARM AFTERNOON

As is usually the case, as soon as the "Fasten Seat Belt" lights go dark, the rush begins: unclick seat belts, get out of chairs, open overhead bins, pull down overstuffed carry-ons without whomping anyone on the head. Then comes the long wait for the plane to pull up to the gate and the doors to open, followed by the exodus.

This time, however. One person stayed on board. She never pulled down her overstuffed carry-on, never opened the overhead bin, never got out of her chair, and never unclicked her seat belt. Somewhere over the Atlantic, she had gone into a coma and nobody noticed. The coma lasted twelve years.

One warm afternoon at the Assisted Care facility

where she was "living" her eyes opened and she screamed. "Help! Call the police! Someone help me!"

Attendants and nurses came running. They all knew Rita. They all had taken turns with her daily sponge bath. They all were there the day the OB/GYN did the C-section and her baby girl was born. They all wondered whether her friends and family even cared after all this time. And they had all given up expecting her to ever return to consciousness.

The resident physician asked her, "Why should we call the police?"

"Because Billy's trying to kill me!"

"Who is Billy?"

"My husband. We've been married two weeks and are on our way home from the honeymoon."

"How did he try to kill you?"

"He injected me with something; I don't know what it was. I felt the sting and looked down to see a syringe in my arm. Then he put a pillow over my face to suffocate me. A few seconds later, everything got fuzzy mentally, I started hallucinating, and I fell asleep. I'm just now waking up. Where am I?"

"We're in your hometown, Rocky Mount, North Carolina, at an Assisted Care facility."

"What? How long have I been here?"

"Twelve years."

"Twelve years? Where's Billy?"

"Rita, we've never met Billy."

"Hand me my purse, please."

"When you came here, you didn't have a purse. All you had were the clothes you were wearing when the plane landed. Your parents come to visit every Monday."

"What day is it?"

"It's Monday. They should be here in ten minutes."

12
TOO MANY CONS

"I've heard it before, so don't give me any of that crap!"

"Whaddyamean?"

"Same old sob story. I'm innocent. But I'm not falling for it."

"But it's true."

"Yeah, yeah. That's what they all say."

"Whaddyamean?"

"Look. Call me jaded, insensitive, whatever you want, but I've listened to too many cons. I've heard too many lies. I've smelled too many rats. I'm no longer naïve. I know instinctively when someone isn't being honest. I just know."

"You just know, huh."

As they walked the yard, a guard came up to the two of them.

"Which one of you is Johnson?"

"I am."

"We just got word you're getting out. Turns out you really didn't commit the crime after all. Follow me."

"Yamean I'm goin' home?"

"Yup. Your boss is waiting for you in the visitors center."

"My boss?"

"Yup. The guy says he never doubted you and wants you to come back to work."

"You're kidding!"

"You wife is here, too."

"Whaddyaknow! He was tellin' the truth!"

13
Q & A

"May I ask you a question?"
"Sounds important?"
"There are some very famous questions, you know."
"Give me an example?"
"Let's see if I can name a few."

To be or not to be?
Where's Waldo?
What's the meaning of life?
Et tu, Bruté?
Where in the world is the poky little puppy?
Wherefore art thou Romeo?
Who ya gonna call?

If I had another face, do you think I would wear this one?"
What would it profit a man to gain the whole world but lose his soul?

"Why are you suddenly so interested in questions?"
"Like I said, I have a question for you?"
"Sounds serious. What is it?"
"Will you marry me?"

14
BEAUTY QUEEN

It had been three months since the accident and Ashley hadn't looked in the mirror. Not even once. Afraid of what she'd see, she had asked her parents to remove the mirrors from her bedroom and bathroom.

She was a pretty baby. As a young girl and all the way through school, she became even prettier. "Pretty enough to be a beauty queen," her granddad said more than once. In high school she had the interest of every boy and the envy of every girl. In college she met a great guy and after dating a few months, he proposed and she accepted. The accident happened one week before the wedding.

She listened whenever her doctor, her family, or

her fiancé spoke, hoping to get a clue as to whether she looked good or not. It was hard to tell. After her third surgery, they all seemed to select their words too carefully, which caused her to worry she might be ugly the rest of her life.

"Today's the day," she said out loud, even though she was the only one in the room. The only one at home. And as far as she felt right now, the only one in the world.

After getting dressed and putting on a mask, Ashley walked down the hall to her parents' bedroom where her mom had a full-length mirror. She stood there. Gathering the strength to face the truth. Either good or bad. Finally, she removed the mask, looked into the mirror, and cried.

15
SELF-DEFENSE

"Do I need to remind you, Mr. Clinton, that you're under oath?"

"No, you do not. As crazy as this may seem, what I'm telling you is the truth."

"All right, then please tell the court one more time exactly what happened."

"I shot the sheriff, but I did not shoot the deputy."

"But three other witnesses say you did."

"No, like I already told you. I shot the sheriff, but I didn't shoot the deputy, I'm tellin' the truth, man."

"Then how do you account for what they're saying?"

"Everyone in town is trying to blame me. Tryin'

to pin it on me. They all say I'm guilty of killing the deputy."

"And yet you deny it?"

"Yes."

"But you do admit to shooting the sheriff. Why did you shoot the sheriff?"

"Listen. I shot the sheriff, but I swear it was in self-defense. I had to protect myself. That sheriff hated me. Always had somethin' against me. An' I don't even know why."

"You expect us to believe that Sheriff Brown was trying to kill you and you acted in self-defense?"

"Yes, indeed. When he pulled me over, I might have been going a little over the speed limit, like maybe going fifty in a forty-five zone. I swear not a bit faster. All of a sudden I see that sheriff with his gun aimed at me. So, I shot him."

"You killed him?"

"It was self-defense. One hundred percent. Honest to God."

"Is that when the deputy arrived on the scene?

"Yes. I shot the sheriff, but not the deputy."

"Then who did?"

"Someone's lyin' 'cause I didn't do that. Look at the surveillance video. It shows clear as day what happened."

"I told you. The judge already ruled that the video will not be accepted as evidence."

"That makes no sense. There's a security camera that shows in broad daylight what happened. I have my rights."

"If you didn't shoot the deputy, then who did?"

"Had to be somebody else. After I shot the sheriff in self-defense, I put the gun down. It was after I put the gun down that the deputy was shot. It couldn't have been me. Quit messin' with me."

16
BLUE BOUGAINVILLEA

Who's the little boy in this picture?

That's my son.

I didn't know you had a child?

My three-year-old-baby-boy loved flowers. All kinds; all colors. He loved seeing pictures of flowers in magazines and books. We used to take the city bus to the library in the afternoon and he would ask to look at books showing gardens, bouquets, corsages . . . any arrangement of flowers we could find. There was a florist on that bus route, so after spending an hour or so at the library, we'd sometimes get off at the flower shop and he would run and laugh and point to the flowers. He was so little and had to look up to see them, or I had to hold him. And such a charmer that the people who owned the shop sort of adopted him. They'd have candy or ice cream for him. That was my three-year-old-baby-boy.

One day we were at the bus stop and he saw a gorgeous bush across the street. That bush was full of beautiful blossoms: blue bougainvillea. Anyway, he got so excited he ran towards that bush before I could stop him and . . . well . . . That was a long time ago. I'll never forget my three-year-old-baby-boy. Today is his birthday. He would've been fifty-three.

17
SUPERBOWL MVP

Even though they were favored to win, at half-time they were at the wrong end of a fourteen-to-nothing score, and the championship was on the line. Before the game, everybody in the world assumed the star running back would be Superbowl MVP, but he was having a bad game, fumbling three times in the first half. Another player on his team recovered one of the fumbles, but two of the dropped balls were picked up by the other team and returned for touchdowns. In addition to fumbling three times, he just seemed to be ineffective, like his mind was somewhere else.

In addition to a few defensive adjustments, the coach decided to make some changes on offense.

They would focus more on passing than running and they would insert their second string running back. The starter had never been benched in his life. Humiliated, he slammed his helmet to the ground, pacing and cursing on the sidelines during the third and fourth quarters.

The new strategies paid off, though. On the opening drive of the second half, they moved down the field using mostly pass plays. The first time they ran the ball, the back-up ball carrier broke free for a twenty-three-yard touchdown. The defense held the opponent to three and out, and when they got the ball back, the sub ran for thirty yards, seventeen yards, and after a couple of passes, scored again, this time right up the middle for a twelve-yard score.

The fourth quarter was pretty much the same and by the time it was over, the favored team won the game twenty-eight to fourteen.

Their fans went crazy. The second-string running back was named the MVP of the game. Followers of the losing team were disheartened. Players on the winning team were shouting, dancing, pouring Gatorade on the coach, and partying in front of the TV cameras. Players on the losing team walked silently to the tunnel.

In the winners' locker room, the coach and players sprayed champagne, congratulated one another, took pictures, and gave interviews. Some cried, others laughed. Some phoned their friends, families, or lovers.

They all celebrated. One man did not.

18
TWIST OF FATE

It had been four years and ten months since Marty and Kaylee had robbed the bank on the corner of Main Street. They had planned and planned, and then refined and refined the plan a few more times until they were a hundred percent certain it was foolproof. There's no way anybody, not even the keenest minds in law enforcement, would be able to figure out who did it.

"Seven hundred and forty-one thousand dollars!" Kaylee shouted again.

"I still can't believe it," Marty replied.

"How much interest will that bring in?" Kaylee wanted to make sure she understood the impact of their nest egg.

Marty had calculated thoroughly. "If we invest it at five percent, we get thirty-seven thousand dollars in interest the first year. And if we don't withdraw any of the money, it will compound so that the second year it makes thirty-nine thousand. The third year, it's fort-two thousand and it keeps getting bigger. After twenty years, the interest will be about ninety-eight thousand dollars per year, which is more than eight thousand per month."

"And that's when we retire, right?" Kaylee was forty-eight years old and liked the idea of retiring before she was seventy.

"That's right." Marty was a year younger, and just as eager to kiss his working days goodbye.

The money was at a self-storage in Kerrington, Kansas while they waited for the statute of limitations to kick in. Only two more months and then it's all theirs. But Marty was getting antsy.

"What can go wrong?" he wondered aloud.

"Absolutely nothing." Kaylee was sure. "We've gone over this a zillion times. We covered everything, right?"

"Yeah. I know, but . . ."

"But what, Marty? You're not freaking out, are you?"

"I'm just getting nervous is all."

"Well, relax. We did everything right. The money is in fireproof, waterproof ammo boxes. The federal and state statute of limitations is five years, so in two months, there's nothing anyone can do to us. We drive up to Kerrington, get our money, and then start investing. What's there to worry about, hmmm?"

"You're right. Okay, I'll settle down."

But down inside . . . he still worried.

They waited a month after the five-year anniversary of the crime, just to make sure. They stopped for the night in a small hotel in Guthrie, OK. The next day, as they drove north towards Kerrington on Interstate 35, the music on the radio was interrupted by a news bulletin about another potential tornado sweeping through Kansas, but it didn't seem to be where there they were going. Kaylee's excitement increased as Marty's apprehension worsened. When they arrived at the self-storage, they saw that the roof of the building had been ripped off. They went to their unit and found all of their ammo boxes unmolested, so they loaded them into the back of Marty's SUV.

As they pulled onto the road, suddenly two police cars pulled up behind them and two others came from in front of them. Marty stopped at the side of the road and four officers surrounded the car, all four with guns pointed at Marty and Kaylee.

"Get out of the car! Now!" one of the cops shouted.

"What's going on?" Marty demanded.

"A tornado came through here a couple of weeks ago. The insurance company came to inspect everything and secure the stuff stored here, and they noticed your ammo boxes, so they called us to take a look. We installed cameras and have been watching the place to see if anyone shows up. Seems like you're the people who robbed the First Waco Federal Bank five years ago."

"Officer, even if we did that, that was more than five years ago. Isn't there a statute of limitations?"

"You're right. But the statute doesn't apply if someone dies during the crime."

"What are you talking about?" Kaylee interjected.

"Ma'am, you might not know it, but during the robbery the bank manager had a heart attack and died as the thieves made their getaway. That means there is no time limit regarding when you can be prosecuted for the crime. Ironically, had you come a few weeks ago, before the tornado, we would never have known the loot was stashed here, and you'd have gotten away with it. But now, you're both under arrest."

19
IT'S IN MY BLOOD

Jean-Louis was born in Mézel, France, but grew up in Vineland, New Jersey. His parents had moved the family to America in 1884 when he was three, after an unexpected parasite killed all of their vines. His father's family had been the leading vintners in the region for almost three centuries, but after losing the vines, he became bitter, sold the land, and wanted nothing to do with wine or winemaking. Jean-Louis's father was now a production manager at Welch's, overseeing the grape fields for their juice, but for the rest of his life, he was adamant about avoiding wine and all alcohol, just like Mr. Welch.

Jean-Louis, on the other hand, was sick of grape juice, and resented not being able to enjoy some wine once in a while. More than once, during and argument with his father, he shouted, "When I grow up, I'm going to grow my own grapes and make my own wine." Ironically, his parents' had never told him of their family's history of winemaking in the hills around Mézel.

As fate would have it, without telling his parents, during his senior year of high school, Jean-Louis applied to attend Cal Poly San Luis Obispo, a new university on the west coast, and was accepted into their Viticulture and Winemaking program.

"Perfect," he told a friend. "I can escape from my parents and pursue what I really want to do with my life. This is my calling, my destiny, it's in my blood."

20
BANANAS

"Frivolous, I tell you. No truth at all."

"But Mark, people in different places, even on different continents, have experienced it, and they describe it exactly the same. How do you explain that?"

"I don't have to explain it, Fran. It's just preposterous. C'mon! Be reasonable. There's no such thing. Get real."

They'd only been dating a few weeks when the local news station started reporting about people who were found with what looked like their ears melted off the side of their head, eyes shriveled up to about half their normal size, and most of their skin peeled off.

Rumors varied greatly as to what kind of monster

was doing this—everything from beasts that flew, to hideous creatures that followed you and attacked when you were alone—but nobody knew.

When Mark showed up at her condo Friday night for their date, Fran didn't answer the door. He must have rung the doorbell seven or eight times before deciding to call her. Still no answer. He went around back and found the door unlocked. He opened the door and called out her name. Nothing. So he walked in. There in the hall was Fran.

After vomiting, he called 9-1-1.

Fourteen months went by. A year and two months of continued reports around the world, only now, Mark was a believer because he had seen it. He was heart-broken to have lost Fran. Then one day he happened to turn on CNN. Scientists had discovered a deadly, microscopic flesh-eating bacteria that lived only in bananas.

Fran loved bananas.

21
IN-LAWS

Jake needed this job but he had to have his own tools. He knew how to do all kinds of carpentry, but having the right equipment was crucial, and right now he didn't have the money to buy anything and the job was supposed to start next Monday and he really needed a circular saw. But having been without a job most of the past year, credit cards were maxed out, checks were bouncing beyond the roofline, and bill collectors were on a first-name basis.

He and Lizzy had only been married a few years. What started with happiness and hope had soon devolved into sadness because of their situation. They didn't have much hope right now, and certainly couldn't afford to celebrate Jake's birthday next Saturday. Thursday night, Lizzy's mother called and invited them over for lunch the next day.

"Right now's not a good time, Mom. We're going through a rough spot and I'm not sure Jake is up for it."

"Well, honey, you need to eat, so talk about it and let me know, okay?"

"Okay, Mom."

Lizzy ended the call and found Jake in the garage.

"My mom called. They invited us over for lunch tomorrow. Wanna go?"

"No."

"Wanna talk?"

"No."

"We have to eat and we don't have any money and you know they love us."

"But I feel so embarrassed. I hate being with anybody."

"Even family?"

"Yes. Especially family. But hey. You're right. We gotta eat. And they do love you, even though you married a loser."

"Jake, is that how you feel?"

"Yes."

"Well, it's not how I see you."

When they showed up at her parents' home, lunch was on the table, and a nicely-wrapped present sat on the floor in the corner. After they ate, Lizzy's mom brought out a cake. She lit the candles and they all sang Happy Birthday. Then she scooped the ice cream while Lizzy's dad brought the gift to the table. Lizzy had a tear in her eye when Jake opened it and discovered a brand-new skill saw.

22
DANCING TO THE MUSIC

Tommy got home from work around 7:30 and dinner was already on the table. After eating, Maggie cleaned up the kitchen while he showered and got into more comfortable clothes. Several times a week, she put on some music at 9:00, then they danced and made love.

Because the apartment had paper-thin walls and was way too close to the other units in the complex, she turned up the volume of the stereo as high as it could go. The music drowned out the outside world and covered any sounds they might make. The neighbors all heard the music and knew what was going on but they didn't mind because, well, whatever brought a sense of happiness and meaning was worth it, they figured.

At 11:42 p.m. the cops busted down the door and arrested Tommy and Maggie, dragging them out of bed, down the stairwell, out to the squad car. They sped to the precinct, pushed them into separate interrogation rooms, and turned on the spotlights.

It seems ever since they started this tradition five months ago, every time Maggie put the music on loud, someone was murdered in the very place named in the song she blasted to the world. Frank Sinatra sang about New York, New York, and someone was shot in the Big Apple. George Strait asked if Fort Worth ever crossed your mind, and some poor soul bit the dust in Cowtown. On and on, the detectives listed the songs, the cities, and the ways people were killed, and Tommy and Maggie sat there in separate cubicles, stunned, denying they even knew what they were talking about.

"Detective, look, if we're at home listening to music and dancing, what on earth makes you think we could kill someone in Texas or New York or Georgia or Pittsburgh? We're in Seattle for God's sake!" Tommy didn't know what else to say.

"Yeah, we get that. But we did our homework, and we think you're signaling to someone out there who makes a phone call or sends an email and the hit is made. What do you say to that?"

"Well, sir. That's sounds pretty far-fetched, if you ask me. Besides, I don't even know half the songs Maggie plays. It's just mood music to dance and make love, know what I mean?"

"Well, Tommy, we've been doing a little investigating, and we figured out the code, who you work for, and how it all goes down. So, we can do this the easy way or the hard way. It's up to you. Do you want to cooperate or what?"

"Look, I have no idea what you're talking about. Honest."

In the other room, an identical conversation took place. Only in that room, once the detectives told Maggie what they figured out, she simply declared, "I want my lawyer."

23
RUMORS

At 6′4″ and 280 pounds, Victor stood out like a sore thumb in his freshman English class. Even though he was soft-spoken and gentle, most people kept their distance, but they stared. That was inevitable in the ninth grade. They talked about him. That, too, was unavoidable. But mostly they avoided him, which led to a lonely existence, for him.

There are unkind people everywhere, bullies all around the world, and one in particular decided his mission in life was to hurt Victor. Bruce started with insults and name-calling, and subsequently transitioned to taunting. Victor remained calm.

Then came the rumors about Victor and his family, followed by outright lies, fabrication of details that simply weren't true, all designed to get under Victor's skin, but he didn't respond the way Bruce wanted him to. Then came the challenge.

In front of about forty students in the quad outside the cafeteria, Bruce cursed at Victor, insulted his family, called him the stupidest person in the whole school, and told him to get ready for the worst beating he could imagine. Victor turned to Bruce, and for the first time since anybody could remember, Victor spoke.

"Bruce, I know who you are, where you come from, what your circumstances are, and I know what you're trying to do. Do you really want this show-down here in front of everybody?"

"You think you know me, huh. Okay smart guy. Give me my life story."

"You're dad's an unemployed alcoholic who is abusive to your mom and you and your sister. You live in a pretty rough part of town in a run-down house which is why you never have friends over. You're really good at basketball, but you're afraid of failure so you won't even try out for the team. You're smart, but you won't study, so you get bad grades so you can fit in with your friends. You like to intimidate people or beat them up because that makes you feel like a somebody. You like animals and are interested in becoming a veterinarian when you grow up, but your dad makes fun of you and discourages you. Shall I keep going?"

As Victor spoke, Bruce's face was turning redder. He rushed at Victor, arms flailing, curses spewing, tears flowing. Victor deflected the first two swings, spun Bruce around, pulled him into himself, and embraced him so tightly that Bruce could hardly breathe, his arms were pinned to his sides, and his face smashed up against Victor's chest. Bruce squirmed and tried to free himself but couldn't. He was trapped. Immobilized. Powerless.

"Bruce, we could be friends, you know. Being mean isn't the only kind of power. There's physical power, emotional power, intellectual power, and spiritual power. That's what I learned at my church's martial arts program. And the greatest power is love."

Bruce looked up at Victor. Then he closed his eyes, relaxed, and sobbed. Victor held him like that for a long time as the other students gawked and then slowly walked away.

When Bruce finished crying, he opened his eyes and asked, "How did you know all that about me?"

"People talk, Bruce. They talk about you, about me, about everyone. Especially when they think nobody else is listening. Plus, I have the advantage of being multilingual so they think I don't understand. So I've heard a lot about you. And I hurt for you. You have so much to offer."

"Victor, I don't have a real friend. Would you…"

He didn't have to finish the question. Victor released him and held out his hand.

24
LIFE SENTENCE

When the testimonies, presentations of evidence, cross-examinations, and closing arguments were over, the jury sequestered themselves to deliberate, and the judge returned to his chambers to ruminate because the facts of the case were incredibly reminiscent of what his family had experienced and he was traumatized all over again, making it difficult to be objective, and he had a tough choice to make: recuse himself or finish the trial, which he could do, of course, but thinking about it made him wonder if that would be best for the people involved in this case, including himself, and by extension, his wife and kids, which brought a thousand more concerns and a deep angst which he wasn't quite sure how to handle, even after all these years on the bench, leading him to question whether he had ever been the right man for the job, the right man for his wife and family, the right man to enjoy all that life had given him, so he stopped and prayed for forgiveness before removing the pistol from his desk.

25
WORDS OF HOPE

Nobody believed in Ricardo. From the time he was four, he felt disrespected. Nobody expected him to succeed. He wanted to run away or end his life.

But instead of quitting, he studied, disciplined himself, and returned scorn with graciousness. Occasionally, someone would encourage him, and he would write it down. When his notebook contained a hundred messages of motivation, encouragement, or inspiration, he wrote a book titled One Hundred Words of Hope. It became a bestseller and sold 2.3 million copies, leading to interviews and talk show appearances.

Everyone called him an overnight success. But he knew the truth.

26
WORLD'S BEST BURGER

"Did you see the ad on your Facebook feed?"

"That's like asking if I saw the tall guy on the basketball team. Which ad are you talking about?"

"The one about the hamburger contest."

"What? No, I didn't. What did it say?"

"Here, take a look."

"They're having a contest?"

"Yeah."

"For a new hamburger?"

"They want to offer a brand-new item to their menu, and they're going to pay a million dollars to whoever sends in the best recipe. AND there's another million for whoever names the new hamburger."

"Is this for real?"

"Yeah, and I figured with your experience for making the best burgers any of our friends have ever tasted, you might want to enter the contest."

"And you?"

"Well, I'll come up with the name."

"I love it."

"But there's something else."

"What?"

"We've been dating for, like, more than a year now, right?"

"Yeah."

"So, I think maybe we make a deal."

"A deal?"

Yeah, if either one of us wins a million bucks, how 'bout we get married?"

"Wow! I was NOT expecting that."

"How 'bout it?"

"Are you for real?"

"Yeah, you know I love you."

"Well, then. I have a counter proposal."

"Okay . . ."

"Let's do the contest, but why don't we plan on getting married regardless of the outcome?"

"Really?"

"I love you too. We've been saying the only thing holding us back from getting married is the money, but shoot, maybe it's time we realize love is more than money and just make it official?"

"YES!"

He entered the contest online, submitted his

recipe, and waited. And waited.

They got married at the church on the corner, about twenty-eight friends in attendance. Poor, but very happy.

One night as he was grilling burgers, the phone rang. His recipe won the contest. They danced and cried and shouted and made love and drank iced tea because they couldn't afford champagne or even cheap wine.

There would be a news conference the following week to announce it to the world and kick off the second part of the contest.

"Well, Babe? What are you going to call it?"

27
ENGAGEMENT

"Get up! Get up! We're movin' out!"

"What, no Reveille or morning chow?"

"Move it! Scouts just spotted an enemy company comin' this way! We gotta leave now!"

He heard the gunfire getting closer as he threw his gear and the latest letter from his fiancée into his ruck. Before his boots were tied he was dead.

28
IF

One word. That's all it took to unravel a full year of negotiations. Until then, they had been working slowly but surely towards a mutual trust, both sides confident that the other was speaking and acting honestly and in good faith. But suddenly there was a crack in that confidence.

The day they were to sign and finalize the treaty, there was a joint news conference. The two ambassadors stood side by side, smiling. The first got up to speak, expressing gratitude to his counterpart for the work they had accomplished and a heartfelt relief that the war between the two nations would finally come to an end.

After the applause died down, the second

ambassador went to the podium and began similarly. But three minutes and twelve seconds into his speech, he used a word that caused concern. As he spoke, he casually said, "if" we sign this treaty instead of "when" we sign this treaty, and that faux pas unraveled the trust and the confidence that had theoretically been established during the talks.

While the second ambassador continued talking, the first speaker pulled out his phone and texted his president, who gave the order to bomb the other nation's parliament where the members were in session and watching the news conference. They sent a missile to the residence of the president, who was home with his family and a few friends.

29
SEEING IS BELIEVING

When I was nineteen, I was told I needed glasses and I was devastated. All my life I had been under the impression that only wimps, nerds, girls, and old people had to have corrected vision, so for me, this was tragic.

My mother took me to the optometrist, and after waiting forever, it was finally my turn to be humiliated. I couldn't see the letters on the chart. With either eye. Totally embarrassing!

Which is better? A or B? This one or this one? The first or the second?

Over and over until, finally, the doctor told me I was done. He'll call my mom when the glasses are ready.

A month later, we went back to the office to get the glasses and I begrudgingly put them on my face. It felt weird to have these plastic and glass things in front of me. Touching me. Sitting on my nose. They were heavier than I had expected, and I didn't like them at all.

Sitting in the car as we drove home, I looked out at the landscape we passed by.

"Mom?"

"Yes, honey?"

"What are all those things on the trees?"

"Those are called leaves."

"Have they always been there?"

30
THE COIN

"What's that, Charlie?"

"It's a coin of some kind. But I've never seen anything quite like it."

"What does it say?"

"I dunno. It's in Latin or some other language. I have no idea what it says."

"You get that at work like the last fifteen coins and the rest of the stuff you brought home?"

Her voice clearly communicated her displeasure with his bringing home items that he found at work. Or elsewhere, for that matter.

"Yes, I found it in one of the fountains at the zoo. It looks cool, though. I like it."

Charlie and Melinda had a medium-sized home. Three bedrooms, two-and-a-half baths. The den had become Charlie's junk room by default, mostly because of the stuff he brought home from work. No matter what she tried, she wasn't able to persuade him to stop bringing the junk home. It's like he had an addiction. He couldn't not bring it home. He had to have it, had to share it with her, had to add it to "My Collection" as he called it.

"Aren't there some rules or laws that say you can't bring stuff home?" Melinda had asked more than once, hoping that there were.

"Yeah, there are. We have to keep stuff in the Lost & Found for thirty days. Every once in a while, someone will call and ask about what they left behind, but usually we never hear from them. After a month, the boss tells the crew we can take whatever we want, and most of the guys aren't interested."

Most of it seemed worthless, not even worth doing a yard sale or putting it on eBay or The Marketplace. One time, however, he came home with an expensive-looking camera. They looked it up online and ended up selling it for three thousand dollars. They used that money to pay off the car. He found a baseball card that seems to be worth a lot. A rookie card of one of his favorite players when he was a kid. Even though it is in mint condition, he's not interested in selling it. This just served to reinforce his addiction.

A week or so after coming home with the newest addition to his collection, they were in the car at a traffic light on the way to the mall. The light was red for a super long time, much longer than usual.

"What's the matter with it! I wish the light would turn green!" Charlie yelled.

Immediately, the light turned green. But they didn't think anything of it because they had been sitting at the intersection a long time.

The next day, he got a phone call from his neighbor, Bob, who was complaining about Charlie's lawn again. He cited HOA rules and was going to report him. The guy went on and on and on. And after hanging up the phone, Charlie said to Melinda, "I wish he'd just drop dead."

A week went by, and there was an email from the HOA saying there was going to be special election to fill the position that opened when Bob died suddenly of a heart attack.

Every time Charlie made a statement that included the words *I wish,* things happened exactly like he said it." The airport added a runway, even though there was no budget for it. The governor was kidnapped and never heard from again. His baseball team had led the league in losses the past three seasons in a row, but went undefeated the next season. His boss was fired on the spot. At the age of thirty-eight, Charlie grew seven inches taller and Melinda's bust increased four inches.

People died, moved, disappeared, called on the phone, got jobs far away. The weather changed.

Congress made new laws. The HOA disbanded. Their dog, who for years barked way too much, suddenly went mute. That's when Melinda began to realize something was going on. Things happened inexplicably. Almost miraculously.

"Charlie, I've noticed something."

"What's that, Gorgeous?"

"It seems every time you say *I Wish*, it happens."

"What are you talking about?"

She rattled off a list of twenty-five or thirty strange happenings in the past year that they had ignored as coincidences.

"About a month ago, I started making a list of weird things, and the list is pretty long. Then I thought back to when it all started, and it seems to go back to the day you brought that coin home from work."

"That's impossible," Charlie shot back.

"Maybe, but it's happening."

"Give me an example," he demanded.

"Okay. The day after you said you wished you had a college degree because you'd get a raise, there was a letter in the mail from the university awarding you a BS. Charlie, you dropped out after two semesters. But now you're a college graduate and you got the raise?"

"What else?"

"Well, since you asked. Do you know how tall you were when we got married? And how tall you are now?"

"That can be explained scientifically. Delayed Thyroid Activation caused by improved diet."

"So you grew seven inches in one day? No, Charlie. Something weird is happening. I want to look at that coin."

He went to the den and brought it out.

"What does it say?" she asked.

"Let's see if I can make out the words: *Possessoris huius nummi vota eius per quinquennium exaudientur.*"

"What does that mean, Charlie?"

"I wish I knew."

31
THE RIDDLE

Emily just knew it had to be in his library, and she wasn't about to give up just because she hadn't figured it out yet.

"Uncle Cecil and I spent so many hours together in here. It was our favorite place to hang out. We talked. He told me stories. We had lunch in here. He showed me pictures and books and souvenirs from his travels around the world. I practically grew up in here. So, when he died without a will, I knew there would be a note somewhere. I just didn't know it would be a riddle.

"Read it to me again, Emily."

"Okay."

The finder of the key is the person who
Understands the radius of the earth times two
Travel east from this very spot
If you want to have a shot
Look straight down onto the ground
And the answer will be found

"But Emily, the experts have dissected the riddle. They know that the radius of the earth is about 3,959 miles, depending on where you measure and whose numbers you're using. But that's the distance your uncle used in his lectures. When you double that, it comes to 7,918 miles. And exactly 7,918 miles east from here is in the ocean, about 500 hundred miles east of Japan. There's nothing there. Not even a tiny island. Which means there is nothing to the riddle. It's a red herring or a smokescreen." Geoffery was running out of patience.

"No! I know him. I understand that the police might not get it, but I believe Uncle Cecil wrote it for me, and for me only. He knows me and he knows that I know him and how he thinks."

After reading the note again, Emily was certain that the answer to his riddle had to be here in this room.

"But we've looked a dozen times," Geoffery reminded her. "So have the police. You've racked your brain over and over, trying to come up with it. Maybe there isn't an answer. Maybe it's just too hard. Too hard for the police detectives working the case, and too hard for you and me."

"Maybe we're trying too hard. What if it's a lot simpler, so simple that I'm looking past the solution?"

"We'll, I'm going outside to get some fresh air. I have nothing more to offer."

Geoffery and Emily were pretty good as secret agents, but this kind of investigation was different. She wondered if maybe it wasn't detective work or spy techniques that this called for. Instead, it called for something else, something personal. That's it! It required knowing Uncle Cecil personally and knowing his history. Maybe even having a shared history. Could that be it?

Emily sat in the chair behind her uncle's desk. Professor Cecil Underwood, world class historian and traveler. Where would he have hidden the key?

As she sat there looking around the library, her eyes watering, so many memories flooded her mind. So many shared experiences. She looked at the floor-to-ceiling shelving. The art and mementos on the walls, the shelves, and the counters. The books, the papers, the maps, the parquet floor, the antique wooden globe that she used to spin when she was a little girl. Her mother always told her to stop spinning the globe, but Uncle Cecil just winked and when her mother wasn't in the room, said it was okay to do it.

The globe? Maybe the riddle referred to that globe instead of the earth. She took her uncle's measuring tape from the drawer and went over to the globe. She measured the circumference, the diameter, and the radius. The radius was exactly 20 inches. 20 inches times two would be 40 inches. Which way was east? Knowing where he stored his compass, she retrieved it and returned to the globe. She pulled out the tape to 40 inches and lay it straight towards the east and set it onto the floor.

"Aha! There it is!"

Etched into the wooden floor in a manner that blended into the parquetry, was the phrase *Emily's favorite spot*.

She had never told anyone about her favorite spot. Only Cecil knew about it. She ran over to the far corner of the room and opened the lower cabinet door. She used to hide in there when she was three and four and had confided to Uncle Cecil that it was her favorite spot. She looked inside. Taped to the underside of the shelf was a key. A key that she recognized.

She took the key back to the globe, spun it around for old times' sake, then located the slot on the equator in Indonesia, inserted the key, and turned it.

ABOUT THE AUTHOR

Paul Linzey is an award-winning author who completed the Master of Fine Arts in Creative Writing at the University of Tampa with a dual emphasis in Fiction and Nonfiction.

He is a member of several writers associations, was a university Associate Professor of Creative Writing, and is a speaker at writers conferences and author groups. He is currently the president of the Lakeland, Florida chapter of Word Weavers International.

You may see his full list of writings on his website: https://paullinzey.com/ and you are welcome to contact him using the Connect page.

BOOKS BY PAUL LINZEY

Fiction

Bekker's Burial
You Never Know
Twist of Fate

Nonfiction

Safest Place in Iraq
Butterfly Believers
Gotcha
Military Ministry
WisdomBuilt: Biblical Principles of Marriage

Contributing Author or Editor

The Warrior's Bible
Reflections: An Anthology of Memoir & Short Story
Dead in the Water: The USS Yorktown at Midway
Looking Through the Rearview Mirror
Reflections Along the Journey
Getting it Twisted

www.ingramcontent.com/pod-product-compliance
Lightning Source LLC
LaVergne TN
LVHW090614110826
845146LV00001B/391

* 9 7 9 8 9 9 8 5 0 6 0 8 6 *